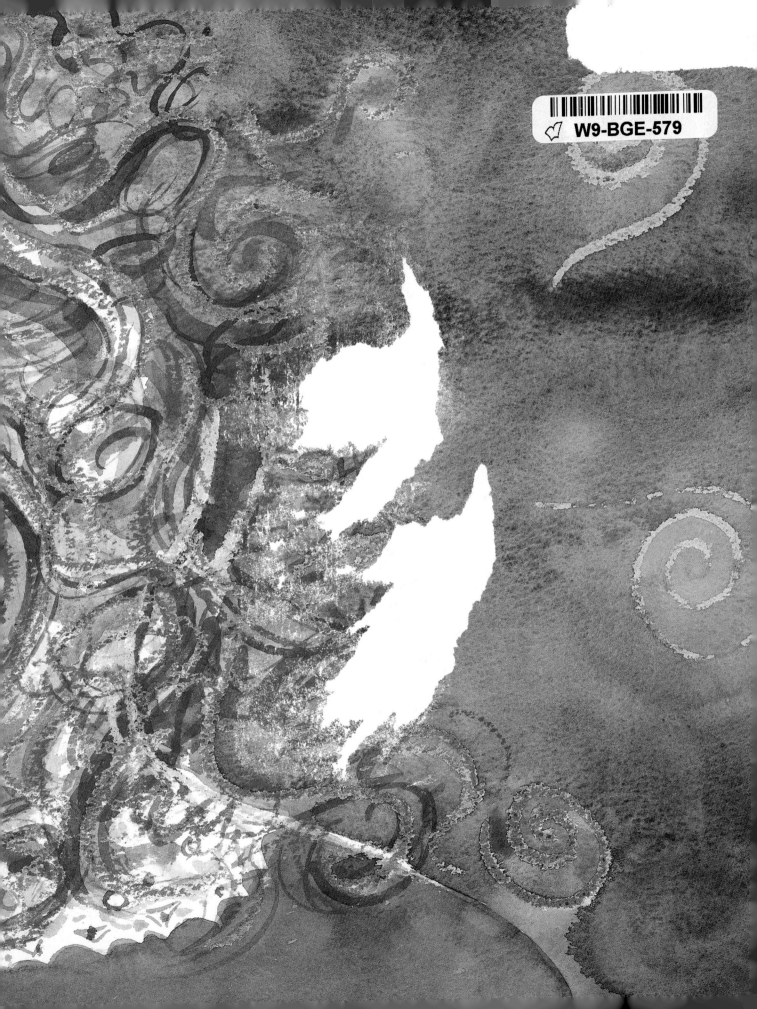

For Clare and Shauna, Mark and Laura - D.C.
For Rachael - B.O'D.
For Niamh - B.E.

Text © 2000 Declan Carville
Illustrations © 2000 Brendan Ellis
Cover Illustrations © 2000 Brendan Ellis

First published in Ireland by Discovery Publications.
Published by arrangement with McGraw-Hill Children's Publishing.
The Author/Illustrator asserts the moral right to be identified as the Author/Illustrator of this work.

 Children's Publishing

This edition published in the United State of America in 2003 by
Gingham Dog Press,
an imprint of McGraw-Hill Children's Publishing,
a Division of The McGraw-Hill Companies.
8787 Orion Place
Columbus, Ohio 43240-4027
www.MHkids.com

Library of Congress Cataloging-in-Publication Data is on file with the publisher.

Printed in Belgium.

1-57768-671-3

1 2 3 4 5 6 7 8 9 10 DSCP 09 08 07 06 05 04 03 02

Kathleen O'Byrne
Irish Dancer

by **Declan Carville**
illustrated by **Brendan Ellis**
book design by **Bernard O' Donnell**

GINGHAM DOG
P R E S S

Columbus, Ohio

Kathleen had a dream. She wanted to be a dancer, but not just any kind of dancer. Kathleen wanted to be an Irish step dancer.

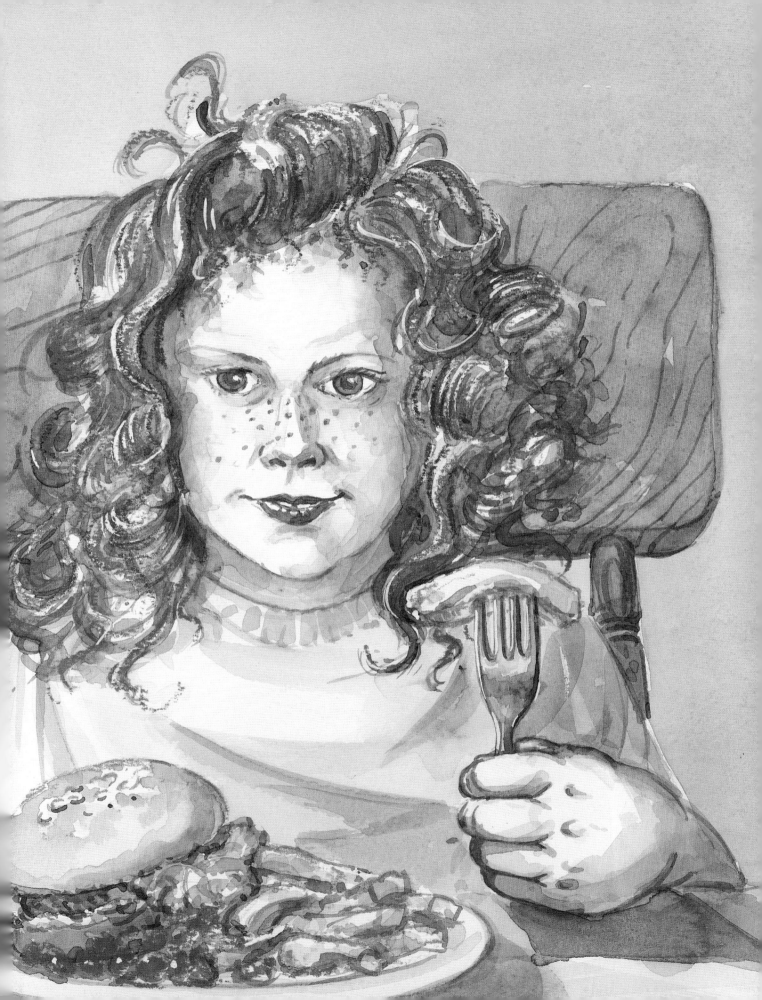

Jigs, reels, and hornpipes—she loved to practice all the different dances. Everywhere. In the kitchen.

In her bedroom.

In the bathroom.

In fact, Kathleen just loved to perform. It didn't matter where.

Even at the bus stop.

Kathleen was especially proud of her dancing costume. She wore it only on special occasions.

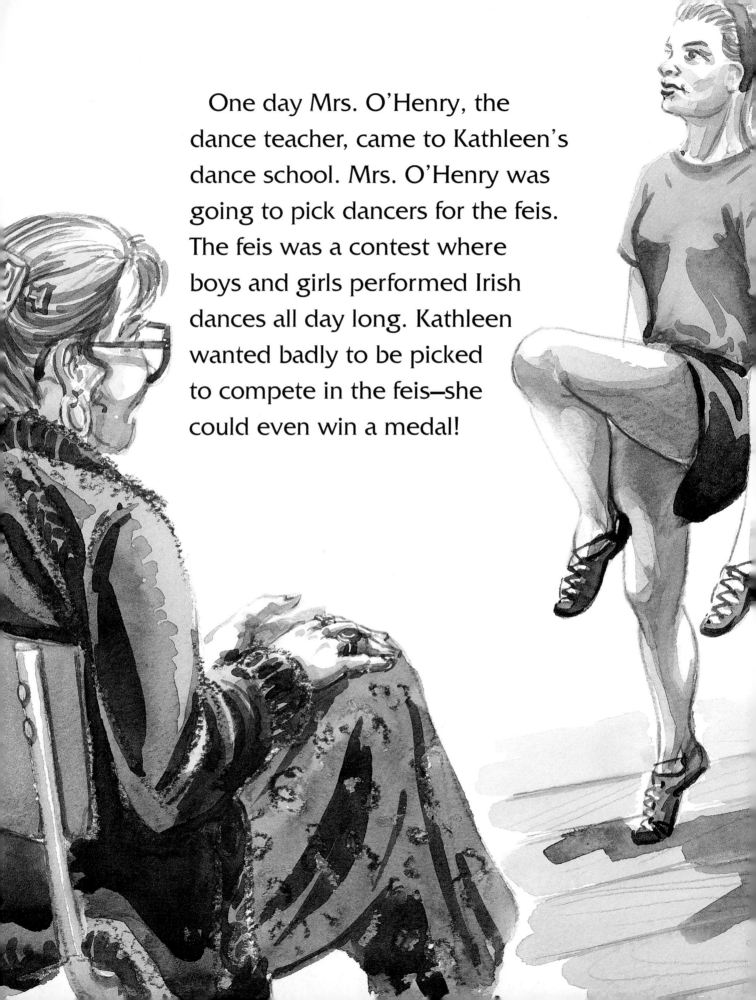

One day Mrs. O'Henry, the dance teacher, came to Kathleen's dance school. Mrs. O'Henry was going to pick dancers for the feis. The feis was a contest where boys and girls performed Irish dances all day long. Kathleen wanted badly to be picked to compete in the feis—she could even win a medal!

"Let's try a slip jig, girls," said Mrs. O'Henry.

Kathleen was so nervous she felt her heart jump, but when the music started to play, she thought about nothing else but her dancing. She kicked her legs as high as she could and kept her arms by her sides. Kathleen felt as light as a feather in her soft shoes.

But Mrs. O'Henry didn't pick Kathleen for
the feis. In fact, she hardly even noticed her.

As Kathleen walked slowly to the bus stop,
she didn't practice her dancing. No twirls or
spins today. It seemed to take forever to get home.

Mom told her there would be another chance next year. She made Kathleen a sandwich. "Go in and sit down, honey," she said. "Your legs must be tired."

Kathleen sank into the chair and turned on the TV. She didn't feel hungry. All she wanted to do was dance.

Just then, she caught sight of some Irish dancers on TV and had an idea. She sat up so quickly her milk nearly spilled on the floor.

"I'll be next door," she called to Mom as she ran outside.

Kathleen knocked on the neighbor's door. "Is Mary here?" she asked Mrs. Walsh. "I need to see her." Mrs. Walsh asked Kathleen to come in.

That night, Kathleen and Mary invited their friends from the neighborhood to a top-secret meeting in the garage, *kids only*. They talked for hours, until it was time to come in for supper.

"Let's meet tomorrow," Kathleen said to the others. "We have lots more to do."

Kathleen and the neighborhood kids met all week long. Finally on Friday, they put up a big poster outside Kathleen's house.

Come to the Show!
Saturday at 1 o'clock
Dancing, Singing, and
Lots More!
Everyone Welcome!

From her bedroom window, Kathleen watched people pass by and read the sign. *Would they all come to the show?* she wondered. That night, she was so excited, she could hardly sleep.

The next day was show day. Mary passed out
tickets until the seats in the backyard were full.

Sean Hughes came out first
and performed his magic tricks.

Then the twins Angela and Claire sang some lively
Irish songs. People in the audience even joined in!

Kathleen came on at the end. She was the last act in the show, but she didn't just walk on. She ran on, legs flying through the air!

She performed one of her favorite dances, a hop jig. Kathleen tried to remember everything she knew. She let her feet be carried away by the rhythm of the music. She kept her hands straight by her sides.

Kathleen danced the best she'd ever danced. It didn't matter anymore that she hadn't been picked for the feis. Not now. What mattered was that she was in front of an audience doing what she loved to do.

When her dance ended, people clapped and cheered. Kathleen took many bows. And as she did, she began planning her next show.

Look at me, she thought, smiling at everyone. *I'm an Irish dancer!*